The Emperor's Teacup

and More Tales from Near and Far

Jacqueline Dembar Greene
Illustrated by April Hartmann

Rigby

Contents

The Emperor's Teacup

Many years ago, the Emperor of Japan lived in the beautiful city of Kyoto. Temples with tiled roofs dotted the land, and the Imperial Palace graced the heart of the city.

It happened that a man named Yamamoto was an expert at recognizing the fine porcelain teacups and teapots used in the Japanese tea ceremony. Serving tea was an art and a ritual. Fine porcelain teacups and teapots were prized possessions that very few could afford to own.

One admiring word from Yamamoto would increase the value of even a tiny teacup at least ten times. He was constantly invited to sip tea with military generals or with important members of government. Yamamoto was a favorite of the emperor himself. The emperor loved nothing better than to have the famous man sitting at his elbow, discussing techniques for glazing fine pottery or admiring the emperor's many tea sets.

One day, Yamamoto stopped at a small tea house for a bit of refreshment. He ordered a pot of green tea and let it steep until its color looked like liquid jade. When he filled his teacup and lifted it to his mouth, he was amused to discover that a small drop of tea had leaked from the cup onto his hand. He wiped it off, being careful not to let it spot his silk kimono.

When he once again felt the hot tea on his hand as he tried to drink, he lifted the cup to the sunlight to discover the problem. Yamamoto smiled to himself as he saw that the rough cup, surely made by an apprentice who had not yet mastered his craft, was poorly glazed. Tea was seeping through the cup's thin walls. With a small grin, Yamamoto left a few coins on the table and went on his way, leaving the tea untouched.

But Yamamoto was so well known that his brief time at the teahouse did not go unnoticed. A workman named Matsui sat on the steps of the porch observing all that had happened. As soon as the porcelain expert left,

Matsui thought he saw a great opportunity.

"How fortunate I am," he thought. "I have just seen the great Yamamoto admiring a teacup. Surely it must be worth its weight in gold." Although he wondered why Yamamoto hadn't purchased it immediately, Matsui knew that this was to his favor.

He called the serving girl and said, "I am afraid that my work today has dirtied my clothes and made me unfit to sit at one of your tables. Please allow me to purchase a cup, fill it with tea, and I shall take it with me as I walk home."

The girl smiled at Matsui and said the cups were of no value, so she would gladly give him one to take along.

"If you please, then," he said, "I would like to have the cup used by the gentleman who just left. He seems a wealthy man, and perhaps some good fortune will rub off on me if I have the cup he used."

The serving girl went off to fulfill Matsui's request, but soon returned with disappointing news. "The master of the teahouse has told me you may choose any cup we have, except for the one you requested. The Master is partial to that one and doesn't wish to part with it."

Matsui had not been the only person who observed the porcelain expert smiling and holding the little teacup to the light. The master of the teahouse had also seen this, and he, too, decided that the cup must be of some value to catch the eye of the famous Yamamoto. He was not going to part with the cup until he determined its value.

But Matsui insisted. "I believe my fortune is tied to that cup," he protested. "I will gladly pay for it. I must have that very one."

The owner came out and began to bargain with Matsui. "I bought that cup as part of a large basket of such cups from a traveling peddler," he said. "It may be of greater value than I realized. I plan to use it for customers of the highest ranks of society."

With that, Matsui unwound his sash and withdrew a few coins. "I must have that cup. How much will you sell it for?"

The owner decided that perhaps this was the best time to make some money from the cup. After all, if it had been extremely rare, Yamamoto would have purchased it. The teahouse master would name his highest price, and if the workman agreed, he would consider himself well paid.

"I cannot part with it for less than one piece of silver," the owner said. Matsui could scarcely afford to give up a month's wages for a teacup, but he pulled the coin from his sash and handed it over. The owner clapped his hands, and the serving girl appeared, holding out the freshly washed cup.

In the privacy of his home, Matsui turned the cup over and over in his hands. He held it to the light, looking for special markings. To his untrained eye it seemed like an ordinary cup, just like any of a million cups in any of a thousand teahouses. But he knew he had a treasure.

The next day, he carefully wrapped the cup in a thick piece of cloth and carried it to a porcelain buyer. "I am here to sell a valuable item," he said as he unwrapped it. "What will you offer me for it?"

The buyer looked it over quickly and declared that the cup wasn't worth the time it took to discuss it. "It's worthless!" he said, and turned away.

Matsui was angry at the man's rudeness,

but decided the buyer was simply ignorant. He wrapped his treasure and went to a second porcelain merchant, but met with the same result. From one shop to the next, Matsui made the rounds, each time growing angrier and angrier. To the very last merchant, he said, "This cup was admired by none other than Yamamoto himself!"

The buyer sniffed as if he smelled something foul. "Then his reputation is not deserved. This cup is refuse from the poorest pottery shop," the buyer retorted.

At this, Matsui felt as if a typhoon had whipped through him. Exhausted from his rounds and filled with shame at being swindled out of a silver piece, he rushed to Yamamoto's home. Clopping across the wooden walkway in his thick sandals, he found the porcelain expert seated in his peaceful garden, admiring a blossoming pear tree.

"Swindler! Thief!" he cried, waving the cup in the air.

"I do not know you," Yamamoto protested. "How could I have cheated you?"

"You admired this cup in the teahouse yesterday. After difficult bargaining, I purchased it from the owner for a piece of silver. And now I am told by every porcelain merchant in the city that it is of no value! You have cheated me with just a glance!"

Yamamoto calmed the worker and offered him a seat on a stone bench in the peaceful garden. After learning his name, Yamamoto spoke to him kindly.

"Matsui-*san*," he said, adding the term that showed respect, "you have paid a heavy price for my reputation. I merely smiled with amusement at the poor quality of the cup. It was so badly glazed that it leaked tea upon my hand."

Yamamoto sighed and continued on. "I have not asked for my fame, but it must be paid for." With that, he took three silver pieces from his sash and handed them to Matsui. "This should pay for your trouble," he offered. "I shall keep this troublesome cup so that no one else is fooled."

As you may guess, Matsui was quite pleased with the outcome of his meeting with Yamamoto. He never expected triple what he had paid for it. Matsui was so pleased with himself that he couldn't help going back to the teahouse to boast of his success.

Sipping a cup of black tea, he caught the owner's eye and beckoned to him with a crooked finger. The owner was suspicious, and spoke with gentle words.

"Good afternoon, Matsui-*san*. I hope that your purchase of the cup has brought you the good fortune you expected."

Matsui smiled. "I sold it to the porcelain expert himself," he boasted. "Yamamoto missed the cup's value when he handled it yesterday. But I showed him its true worth, and agreed to sell it to him for a small price. Since I paid so little for the treasure, I sold it for just three times what I paid for it."

When he saw the owner's startled look, he couldn't help but add, "Of course, you can be sure that Yamamoto has better connections than I. He will surely make much more from it than a poor worker like me." He swallowed the last drop of tea from his cup and walked off, leaving the owner to regret his hasty deal.

A few days later, the owner of the teashop was summoned to the elegant home of Nagoya, a government deputy. Nagoya was planning a party to celebrate his promotion, and hired the owner of the teahouse to pre-pare tea and refreshments for his guests. Because the teacup was still on the owner's mind, he described his recent experience.

"To think that I let such a treasure slip from my hands," he said. "If I still had the cup, I would surely use it when I prepared the tea ceremony for your respected guests."

After the teahouse owner left, Nagoya imagined the admiration he would receive if he owned the cup. Everyone would speak of his intelligence. They would admire his ability to purchase such a collector's item. They would whisper about his knowledge of fine porcelain. He decided that he must own the cup.

He headed straight to Yamamoto's house, and was prepared to pay any price. Yamamoto looked through his window and saw his visitor was none other than Nagoya, a boastful man whom Yamamoto thought a fool. He disliked men who thought more of their possessions than of their manners. But he answered the door.

Nagoya did not bow or offer a simple courtesy of any kind. This only deepened

Yamamoto's bad feelings for the man.

"I have heard of a wonderful cup you recently purchased," Nagoya said, "and I beg you to sell it to me."

Yamamoto did not wish to swindle the man, no matter how much he disliked him. "It is a thing of no value whatsoever," he explained. "It is merely an ordinary cup."

"Don't try to fool me," Nagoya argued. "I have no interest in your games. Whether or not you deserve your reputation of being a porcelain expert, I must deal with you on this matter. To me, you are nothing but a merchant of silly tea things. Since you have what I wish to buy, sell it to me without wasting my time."

Yamamoto was greatly insulted. Now he felt Nagoya deserved whatever he lost in the deal. He used sweet words on his annoying neighbor.

"Ah, Nagoya-*san*," he said, "you are a man of action. I will tell you then that this cup has a rare feature. Although no flaw can be seen in it, it gives off the slightest drop of liquid when it is filled."

The eyebrows of the foolish neighbor lifted

with interest. Yamamoto directed his house servant to bring the cup and a pitcher of water.

As Nagoya watched with amazement, Yamamoto filled the cup and then handed it to his neighbor. In a moment, a drop of water fell onto Nagoya's thumb.

"I must have this magical vessel," he declared. "It is a treasure that will not be found again. Perhaps I judged you too soon, Yamamoto. You do have a good eye for these trinkets."

Now Yamamoto had Nagoya exactly where he wanted him. "I hate to let it go," he said, pretending to be unwilling to part with it. "But you are a wealthy man, Nagoya-*san*, and I am but a lowly seller of tea things." He hesitated a moment. "I will let you have it for 500 gold coins."

Nagoya was overjoyed. He told Yamamoto his servant would be sent over immediately with the payment. He held the precious cup in his hands and headed home before the porcelain expert changed his mind.

The next evening, Nagoya entertained his guests with a lavish buffet. Then he spoke to them about the marvelous teacup he had just acquired. He pretended to have an eye for rare pottery. He pretended the discovery of the cup was his alone. He gave a demonstration of the cup's magical ability to produce a dewy drop of moisture when it had no crack and no hole in it at all. His guests applauded this little show.

Afterward, the secretary to the prime minister spoke to Nagoya. "My master loves collecting unusual pieces. It's a shame he isn't here to witness your demonstration."

Nagoya saw a new opportunity. Perhaps the cup would help him toward a better job. "I would love to present this teacup to the prime minister. Please tell him it is a pleasure for me to give it to him."

Although he had paid an enormous sum for the cup, Nagoya thought of it as an investment in his future. If the prime minister looked upon him with favor, there was no end to the promotions he might receive.

He wrapped the cup in a piece of fine silk and placed it in a velvet-lined box with a note to the prime minister. Then he sent it on its way, certain that he had secured his own fortune with the gift.

But when the prime minister opened the box, he barely glanced at the cup. He said to his secretary, "I have no interest in pottery." Then he had an idea. "It might be of interest to the emperor, though. He collects such things. I have been summoned to meet with him on Thursday. Now I have a gift that is worthy to bring."

Since life is filled with unexpected happenings, it came to be that when the prime minister presented the cup to the emperor, who but Yamamoto was sitting at his side.

"What do you think of this piece?" the emperor asked the porcelain expert. "I don't recognize its design or its shape as anything I have seen before. I will rely on your expert opinion."

Yamamoto began to laugh. He laughed until his sides shook. "Your Majesty," he said, when he could catch his breath, "forgive me. But there is a story here that I think will greatly entertain you." With that, he began to weave the tale of the little teacup, beginning with the moment he first drank from it in the teahouse.

When Yamamoto reached the end of his

tale, the prime minister told him how the cup had been given to him. The emperor enjoyed a hearty laugh with his guests. He took the cup and turned it over in his hands.

"Well, Yamamoto, you are the man who set this little cup upon its journey and established its value. I see you tried to be honest about it, but events were out of your hands."

Then the emperor took a brush and ink and signed his name on the side of the modest cup. He placed it in the box and presented it to Yamamoto. "The cup surely belongs to you," he said.

And so it happened that Yamamoto, the famous porcelain expert, came to own the most valuable teacup in all of Japan. With the signature of the emperor written on its side, the teacup was indeed priceless.

Victory for the Victim

Menelik lived high on the plateaus of Ethiopia, helping his family grow beans and peas on their small piece of land. But for two years in a row, the rains did not come, and neither did the crops. Menelik and his parents grew lean, and they owned only a few scrawny chickens and one nanny goat.

One morning, Menelik's father looked out over the dry fields and the withering plants.

"My son, you must go from this parched place," he said. "Perhaps you can find a new home where the earth is rich, and the rains water the crops."

Menelik did not want to leave his family. But he thought his parents might be better off with one less mouth to feed. His mother wiped away her tears and told him not to worry. Someday, when life was better, they would be together again.

15

His father placed a chicken in a basket and tied it on the back of the nanny goat. His mother gave him a calabash gourd filled with sweet water and some thin bread called *injera*.

"Let the goat graze when you find greener fields," Menelik's father told him. "Then every morning you will have fresh milk to drink and an egg from the chicken." With his heart feeling like lead and his belly like an empty drum, Menelik left home.

Along the dusty path he walked, his bare feet leaving their marks behind him. By the end of the day, he had left his stone house far behind. He came to a meadow with a small stream. Menelik tethered the nanny goat to a wooden stake and watched her graze hungrily, devouring grass and weeds. Menelik ate, too, gulping his water in just a few swallows, and allowing himself one piece of *injera*.

The next morning, he built a small fire and roasted the egg under the ashes. He milked the goat, filling his gourd. He picked up a long, straight stick from the ground and used it as a walking staff as he set forth. "I have left hunger behind me," he vowed, "and I am going forth to life." He marveled at the different sights around him, for he had never traveled farther from his door than the fields he tended.

As the day turned to dusk, Menelik came upon a man pulling a goat from a well. He stopped to help, tugging on the rope with all the strength he had left. When at last the goat was standing on land, Menelik questioned the man.

"May I spend the night here, and fill my gourd with water?" Menelik asked.

The man smiled, showing crooked teeth. "My friend, I would share with you whatever water I had, but this is not a drinking well. It is a goat well."

Menelik was amazed at the man's words. "I have never heard of a goat well before."

The man rubbed the stubble on his chin and thought for a moment. "I suppose that isn't surprising," he said. "There are only a handful of these goat wells in Ethiopia. Any well can produce water if you dig deep enough. But a goat well—that is a special thing."

Menelik's nanny goat and the man's goat nuzzled each other. "At night," he said, "I toss in two goat horns. In the morning, there is a goat at the bottom of the well. I climb down carefully, tie a rope around its middle, and then haul it up." He wiped his forehead. "It isn't so easy."

It sounded very easy to Menelik. He imagined that if he had such a well, he could collect a herd of goats. They would bring a good price in the marketplace, and he could buy food for his family whenever the crops were poor. Perhaps this discovery would bring a change in his fortune.

"How much would you ask for this goat well?" he began.

Again the man rubbed his unshaven chin. "How can one put a price upon such a wonder?" The man turned to walk away, and then stopped and turned back. "I have thought about moving to the city of Keren," he said. "How much would you offer for the well?"

Menelik shrugged. "I have only the goat you see here, and this poor chicken. Their milk and eggs have sustained me since I left my home. They are all I have in the world."

"That is nothing. The well can give me a

goat every day, and then I can buy all the chickens I want." Then the man sighed, as if he were burdened with a heavy decision. "But I want to join my family in Keren," he said, "and you look like you need a fresh start in life. Your legs are as thin as twigs. How can you walk any further upon them? Give me your poor goat and your scrawny chicken. I wish you luck." He tossed Menelik two old goat horns. "Here," he said, "this should get you started tonight."

Menelik was overjoyed. "Tell me, my friend, what is your name?"

"They call me 'Where I Can Dance,'" the man called over his shoulder. He wasted no time setting off for Keren with the two goats and Menelik's chicken.

"If I come to good fortune in the future, I promise to share my rewards with you," Menelik called after him.

In no time, Menelik was alone with his thoughts, and so excited about the treasures to come from the goat well that he could barely swallow his last piece of *injera*. As soon as the sun faded, Menelik dropped the goat horns into the well. He curled up on the ground next to it, and praised Where I Can Dance before he fell asleep. Imagine Menelik's disappointment when he awoke the next morning to find the two old goat horns still sitting at the bottom of the well.

"Where is my goat?" he cried. His growling stomach reminded him that not only was he missing his nanny goat, but there was no egg to cook, either. As weak as he was from the hunger gnawing at him, Menelik scoured the fields collecting old goat horns. At night he tossed them all into the bottom of the well. Surely there were at least two horns that would produce the magic that was needed.

But in the morning, nothing rested at the bottom of the well except the horns he had thrown in. There was no bleat of a goat.

At last, Menelik knew he had been swindled. "How could I know so little of the world as to believe that a dry well could produce a goat?" he chided himself. "I will find the man who cheated me, and make him pay!" He picked up his walking stick, and pounding it into the earth with every weak step, he walked until he reached the next village.

"Excuse me," he said to the first man he met there. "Do you know Where I Can Dance?"

The man shrugged. "Anywhere you like, my brother," he said.

"No, no," Menelik protested. "I'm trying to find Where I Can Dance."

A few more people stopped on the street and pointed to the smooth stones beneath Menelik's feet.

"This is as good a place as any," they laughed. A few began to clap their hands. "Come, entertain us with your dancing. Perhaps you can earn a few coins to pay for a meal. You certainly look like you could use one!"

Menelik was so angry with the people that he did not stay another minute. He traveled without stopping until he came to the next village. He nearly collapsed at the well in the center of town. He was barely able to draw a bucket of water to drink before he fell asleep next to it. When he awoke, a group of women stood around the well, balancing jugs on their heads.

"Look, someone has beaten us to the well this morning," laughed one young woman. "I think we must have slept too long, sisters." Giggles erupted all around him, and Menelik felt his face grow warm with embarrassment.

"Excuse me, ladies," he said, bowing. "Have any of you heard of Where I Can Dance?"

One woman placed her jug on the ground and leaned toward him. "Dance, you say? It looks to me as if you should be looking for a place to eat!"

"No, no!" Menelik protested. "You don't understand. I must find Where I Can Dance."

"Why, you poor boy," crooned one of the women. "You can dance anywhere you like." And the women filled their jugs.

Menelik left this village, too. He was so hungry that he thought his throat had forgotten how to swallow. His stomach was too empty to even growl at him. He leaned more and more heavily on his walking stick, until he came to the city of Keren.

Here was a city filled with more people than Menelik had ever seen in one place. The market was so vast that stalls of fruits and vegetables stretched as far as he could see. He became dizzy with the swirl of people, the strong smells, and the bright colors all around him. Just as he was going to ask about Where I Can Dance, a crier came through the streets, shouting to one and all.

"Hear me! Hear me!" he shouted in a singsong voice. "The chief has lost his golden ring. If anyone shall find the ring that bears the chief's seal, a rich reward shall be paid for its return."

The crier's words rang in Menelik's ears,

but he was too weak to think. He slumped to the ground at the edge of the market, and a passerby tossed him a coin.

"They think I am a beggar," he thought sadly. "I hoped to seek my fortune in the world, but I should have stayed home and starved with my parents. At least I wouldn't be alone."

Just then a bright glitter of light caught Menelik's eye. Beside him, gleaming in the hot sun, was a piece of gold. He picked it up, thinking perhaps he had found another coin. When he lifted it from the dust, he realized that it was a gold ring. He wiped it clean against his tattered robe and saw a mighty lion carved upon it.

"Now my calabash is empty of water, and empty of bad luck!" he cried. Menelik wasted no time presenting himself at the gates of the chief's palace. A burly guard stood at the heavy door.

"Go away!" he growled. "No beggars allowed."

"I must see the chief," Menelik stammered.

The guard pulled himself up to his full

height. He seemed as large and powerful as an elephant. "No one gets past me without being summoned by the chief," he said.

"I have found the chief's ring," Menelik said weakly. "I must return it to him."

"You'd best give it to me," the guard snapped. "I will give it to the chief for you." But Menelik was not about to be tricked a second time.

"If you let me pass," he bargained, "I will give you half of the reward I receive." The guard grunted.

"Don't try to trick me," he warned. "You'll never leave this city without keeping your promise." Then he pushed open the creaky door.

Menelik stepped into a bright garden. Pomegranates and lemons grew from the trees. The sweet smell of pears and oranges perfumed the air. He followed a smooth path toward a large stone palace and entered slowly, looking all around him. His dusty feet glided across polished marble floors. Fountains dripped bubbling water into tiled pools. A tall man dressed in woven linens ushered Menelik before the chief. Menelik dropped to his knees and bowed his head to the floor.

"Rise up, young man," the chief ordered. "I am saddened to see someone from my country who has suffered such famine. Have you come to ask for help? If so, I grant it to you."

Menelik shook his head. "It's true that my village's fields have dried up, and there is almost nothing to eat. I left with only a goat and a chicken, hoping to find a better fortune. But along the way, a man swindled me out of my only possessions. He sold me a well that was supposed to produce goats. What a fool I was. The man said his name was Where I Can Dance, but when I've asked for him at each village along the way, people only mocked me."

"Such a deed should not go unpunished," the chief said. "I think I have heard of a stranger who came to town a few days ago leading two goats and carrying a chicken." He summoned a guard and whispered in the man's ear before sending him on his way.

Then Menelik opened his hand and displayed the ring upon his palm. "I believe I have found your lost ring," he said.

The chief's eyes were dazzled at the sight. He took his ring and placed it upon his thick finger, savoring the moment.

"I promised a reward for the return of this ring," he said. "Tell me, my son, what reward would make you the happiest?"

Menelik fidgeted before the chief's steady gaze. "If you can find this scoundrel, Where I Can Dance," he began, "and if you can send for the giant of a man who guards your gate, then I shall ask as my reward 100 days in prison."

"Why, you don't deserve punishment," the chief protested. "I mean to reward you handsomely."

"I thank you for your generous offer," Menelik said, "but I have made two promises. First, I promised Where I Can Dance that I would share my profits with him if I became successful. Then, when I arrived at the gate, your guard refused to let me pass unless I promised to give him one-half of my reward. Therefore, I ask that you reward me with 100 days in prison. Half of them shall be given to Where I Can Dance, and half belong to the guard."

The chief let out a laugh. "Your hunger has not made you any less clever. There are too many times when a man suffers from another's meanness. This time, it will be a reward to see the victim take a small victory."

The chief saw to it that the two men were punished. But instead of being sent to prison, the swindler was banished from the city and the guard was removed from his post. Menelik was housed in the palace, fed nourishing soups and stews until his strength returned, and then brought before the chief once again.

"You have asked for no other reward," he said, "but I shall not send you on your way empty-handed." He clapped his hands, and a line of men entered, each carrying a basket upon his head. "You shall return home with grain and beans and fruits for your family and your village," he said. "There are sacks of seeds to plant crops again. The bag of gold coins is my gift to you. May they sustain you in an honest life with your family."

And so it happened that Menelik returned home to his family in the stone house at the edge of the fields, and was welcomed by the entire village. For the rest of his days, he remembered how his calabash had been emptied of bad luck, and how a victim had won a victory, after all.

Spider Grandmother and the Footrace

In the time of the first Hopi people, two villages nestled side by side. Tikuvi was a large village with acres of cornfields and many men to work them. Payupki was tiny, but the people had everything they needed, and lived a peaceful life.

One day the Payupki chief passed his neighbors in Tikuvi and saw men running races. He saw that the Tikuvi village had swift runners and knew they would become faster the more they trained. When he returned to his own village, he sent for Running Deer, a young boy who had proven himself to be the fastest messenger. The boy could run for hours without tiring.

"Running Deer," the chief said, "Tikuvi men are practicing their racing. I believe they will challenge us to a footrace when they feel they can win. You are our fastest runner. Go to Tikuvi and ask to practice with them. Watch carefully and test them, but do not reveal how fast you can run."

When Running Deer arrived in Tikuvi, he was welcomed among the runners. He competed in the longest footrace so he could see how strong the runners were and who would tire first.

The footracers started the contest with a burst of speed. Running Deer was far behind the pack. He kept his pace steady, and tried to watch while he ran. Soon the men from Tikuvi began to tire. As they fell back panting, Running Deer moved ahead. Soon there were just two runners in front of him. He easily passed the second one. When he was close on the heels of the lead runner, he knew he could overtake him. But Running Deer remembered his task. He was not in Tikuvi to show his greatest skills. He slowed his pace and allowed the man to win the race.

When he returned to his own village, Running Deer talked with the chief. "I came in second," he said, "but I believe I could have won easily if I had run as fast as I could."

"That is what I needed to know," the chief said. "I believe Tikuvi will challenge us to a race soon. You must practice to make yourself even stronger and faster."

Each day, in the cool of morning and in the shadows of evening, Running Deer trained. He ran across the flat mesa, high above the desert floor. He climbed down to the fields where the cattle grazed and ran across the packed sand of the desert. He raced to the hills and ran up and down their changing slopes.

One day the chief of Tikuvi called upon the chief of Payupki. The two men sat together in the *kiva*, the structure where sacred ceremonies and council meetings were held.

"In four days, Tikuvi will hold an inter-tribal race. Come and join us with your best runners, and we shall offer prizes to the village with the swiftest runner."

"My village is small," the Payupki chief said. "We have just one racer, the young boy you have seen. But we shall come and enter him in the race."

The night before the race, the chief of Tikuvi called the village leaders to the *kiva*.

They argued about whether or not it was wise to offer their possessions as prizes in the race. But the chief was not concerned.

"You have seen their best runner already," the chief reminded them. "Running Deer was not able to win when he practiced with us. He will do no better in the race."

While they were talking, Spider Grandmother came down to the ladder in the *kiva*.

"Go away," the men called. "It is only men who are meeting here."

Spider Grandmother tried to ignore their insult. "I have come to help our runners win the race."

But the men were no longer worried. "We don't need your advice," they said. "Go away, Grandmother."

"When you need me, I am always willing to help. Now you tell me to leave. And that is what I shall do." She gathered her few possessions and left the village.

But the men of Tikuvi took no notice. They were busy preparing for the race, planning which men would run, and asking the women to prepare a celebration feast.

Spider Grandmother walked until she came to Payupki. The villagers welcomed her and led her to the *kiva*. Here the leaders were also discussing the race, and their runner's chances. When they saw the old woman coming down the ladder, they called to her.

"Come and join us, Grandmother. What has brought you here?"

She spoke to them honestly. "I tried to help the men in my village find ways to win the race. But they do not want advice from an old woman. They told me to leave. So I have come to offer my help to you."

The chief thanked her. "What advice do you have for us now, Grandmother?" he asked.

"The people of Tikuvi will celebrate tonight. They are certain of their victory. Tomorrow they will be tired. Make sure that your runner sleeps," Grandmother replied.

"You are wise, Grandmother," the chief told her. "We shall do what you say."

When the meeting was over, the leaders found a place for Grandmother to stay. Villagers brought her gifts of warm blankets, cooking pots, and corn. They stacked wood,

and started a fire to keep her warm.

The next morning, the men and boys of Payupki went to the racing grounds. Running Deer walked ahead of them all. A young man collected the things that the villagers brought for the prizes. Arrow points, beaded moccasins, blankets, deer bone necklaces, and scarves lay in a pile. Whichever village won the most races would get everything.

Running Deer raced all day. He ran against Tikuvi runners in long-distance runs. He ran against their best runners for short distances. In every race, Running Deer came in first. The men from Payupki cheered, while the men from Tikuvi scowled. The Payupki men tossed Running Deer into the air.

When the feast had ended, the Payupki villagers collected the goods they had won. When they returned home, they placed the winnings in front of Spider Grandmother and allowed her to choose whatever she wished. Then they gave some of the winnings to Running Deer. The rest were distributed to everyone in the village.

When the new day came, the chief of Payupki called for Running Deer once again. "The men of Tikuvi are poor losers," he said. "I know they will challenge us to another race as soon as they think they can win. You must not let your success yesterday make you soft. You must train even harder to be ready for the next race."

Running Deer rose before dawn each day and ran through the village, through the fields, and across the mesa.

One morning, when he returned to his family, his sister said, "I have watched you, and you are slow. You must learn to run faster. Tomorrow I will run with you and help you."

The next day, Running Deer and his sister raced. And every day she called back to him as she ran by him easily. "Keep your head up, Brother. Hold your back straight, Brother. Use your legs, my brother." They ran on the same course each day, yet when Running Deer finished, he found his sister already back at the house grinding corn.

"Aren't you tired?" he asked.

"That was nothing," his sister said. "I can run faster than that."

In time, the chief of Tikuvi again met with the chief of Payupki. Once again, he invited Payupki to intertribal races. "We must have a chance to win back what we have lost," he said. When the chief of Tikuvi had left, Running Deer met with his village chief.

"We are again counting on you to be the fastest runner," the Payupki chief said. But

Running Deer only shook his head.

"I am not the fastest runner in the village," he explained. "I have been training with my sister, and she is always ahead of me. She must be the one to race for us."

And so the villagers of Payupki sent a message to Tikuvi. "In four days, we shall come to race with you. But our runner will be Running Girl."

The women in both villages were pleased. They would all go to see Running Girl challenge the men. It would be a festive day.

But the men of Tikuvi were nervous. "If our neighbors have a faster runner than Running Deer, how will we be successful against her? Running Deer has already beaten our swiftest racers. We must send for Spider Grandmother and ask for her help." But Spider Grandmother's house was empty. They didn't know where she had gone.

The village of Payupki brought Spider Grandmother into the *kiva* and gave her gifts of food. Then they asked for her help, and she willingly gave it.

"The people of Tikuvi are poor losers," she said. "They are planning to cheat to be certain they win. I will turn myself into a spider, and sit on Running Girl's ear. I will watch for signs of danger and help her."

When the day of the race came, everyone from the two villages stood at the edge of the racing grounds. Men piled up their prizes of arrow points, bows, quivers, and moccasins. Women offered clay pots, blankets, baskets, and strings of turquoise beads. It seemed there was a small mountain of gifts.

Running Girl set her moccasins aside. She tucked her skirt into her belt. When the first race began at midday, she swiftly took the lead. She ran past barrel cactus, their blossoms leaning toward the sun. She ran past formations of rocks that were jutting from the desert. But most of all, she ran past every runner from the village of Tikuvi. The second race ended just like the first.

Before the third race began, the people of Tikuvi knew it was their last chance to win. They chose their fastest runner and decided that he alone would race against Running Girl. Everyone stood along the starting point to cheer them on. This time, Spider Grandmother sensed trouble. She turned herself into a tiny spider and sat on Running Girl's ear. When the race began, she urged her on. "Faster, Granddaughter! Run faster!"

Running Girl flew like the wind, and soon she couldn't see the Tikuvi runner behind her. Over her head, a dove soared through the air.

"So," Spider Grandmother said, "their runner has turned into a dove. He will fly to the finish to beat you."

Spider Grandmother called to a hawk. It swooped down and chased the dove away.

40

Running Girl sped past. But the dove soon returned. The sound of beating wings reached Running Girl's ears. Again, Spider Grandmother called the hawk, and again it chased the dove away. Running Girl raced toward the finish.

As she came within sight of the cheering crowd, the dove turned himself back into a man. Try as he might, he could not overtake Running Girl. The race was over, and Payupki had won again.

All during the feasting that followed, the people of Tikuvi were glum. They did not like to lose. Nothing seemed worse than losing a racing festival, except losing twice. They watched jealously as the people of Payupki collected their winnings.

That night, as the chief offered the first gifts to Spider Grandmother and Running Girl, the old woman spoke to the village. "I can hear the people of Tikuvi plotting against us," she said. "They plan to take back all their winnings. They are preparing for war against us."

The peaceful villagers of Payupki were afraid. "We have too few men to fight," they said. "What can we do?"

"We must leave this place tomorrow," Spider Grandmother said. "I will lead you to a place where we will live in safety."

That night, the people tied their belongings into bundles. They wrapped their cooking pots and grinding stones in their blankets. Mothers tied their babies against their backs. Before the first light of day, they began their journey. Behind them, nothing was left in the village, not even a feather.

Spider Grandmother led them down the mesa, along a trail that they had never seen before. They traveled with their cattle before them, across the canyon, stopping only to fill their water gourds and to let the cattle drink from the streams. For four days they walked, leaving their jealous neighbors behind.

At last, Spider Grandmother led the people to a new site near a running river. They built a new village there, giving the best house to Spider Grandmother and the next best to Running Deer and his sister, Running Girl. They named their new village Payupki in honor of the village they left behind, and forever lived there in peace.

Juan Miguel Sees Three

Juan Miguel lived with his mother and his nine brothers and sisters in a village in Spain. His mother worked hard washing her neighbors' laundry to earn enough to feed her children.

Juan Miguel was the eldest, but instead of helping his mother by chopping wood for the fire that boiled the wash water, he played tricks on his friends. Instead of helping to wring out the wet laundry or hang the clothes to dry, he practiced his tricks. Each day he slept late, and when he finally roused himself, he sat around perfecting his tricks.

"I am so clever," he announced, "that I will go into the world and make my fortune." He promised his mother he would return someday with enough money to take care of the whole family.

To tell the truth, Juan Miguel's mother

wasn't sorry to see her son leave. He was no help at all, and now she had one less mouth to feed. She wished him good luck, and turned back to her work.

Juan Miguel traveled to the first village where people didn't know what a trickster he was. He sat down in the market square and invited passersby to play a game of Find the Pea. He set a dried pea under one of three walnut shells, quickly moved them into different positions, and asked for one *peseta* if the player couldn't guess which shell hid the pea. No matter how carefully the villagers watched, Juan Miguel was too quick for their eyes. Each time they placed a *peseta* on the table, certain they could outwit him, Juan Miguel fooled the player again and pocketed the coin. Soon there was a buzz of anger whenever Juan Miguel set up his game.

"He must be a wizard," one man whispered. Others heard the rumor and added to it.

"Yes, I'm sure this Juan Miguel uses magical powers to make the pea disappear." It didn't take long before Juan Miguel found that no one was willing to play. He moved on to the next town to find new people to trick.

There, he set himself up in the marketplace wearing a flowing blue robe and a silk turban he purchased along the way. He liked pretending to be a wizard. For two *pesetas,* he promised to make the pea under the shell disappear, then reappear where he chose. People flocked to his stall, where he sat regally on a tall stool before a barrel holding the shells. One day, a man placed three *pesetas* on the barrel.

"If you are a wizard," he said, "tell me whether my crops will be bountiful this year, and whether I should plant wheat or tomatoes."

Juan Miguel closed his eyes. He rubbed his temples. He moved his hands mysteriously in front of his face. At last he spoke.

"Rain will come and crops will grow.
Tomatoes and wheat, both you must sow."

The man went away, thinking he had spent his *pesetas* wisely.

"Now I know the future," the man boasted. Days stretched into weeks, and Juan Miguel pretended to see what the future would be for others. He always spoke in rhymes and riddles, and made certain that he would be long gone before any of his predictions could be proven false.

As spring stretched into summer, Juan Miguel decided it was time to leave the village. He hired a tailor to sew stars and shimmering pieces of shell on his robe, fashioned himself a long walking staff, and headed to the city of Seville.

Along the way, he helped himself to plump grapes in the vineyards. He plucked tomatoes from the fields. When he reached Seville, he stopped at an inn and announced that he was Juan Miguel the Great who saw the future and could see into everyone's past.

The innkeeper looked into his deep, dark eyes and decided to treat this stranger with respect. She gave him her finest room, piled his plate with the choicest morsels of food at every meal, and spread the word that Juan Miguel the Great rested at her inn.

It happened that at the very time Juan Miguel was boasting of his powers, all the silver plates and goblets at the castle disappeared. The king was enraged. How could he eat his meals from ordinary plates from the potter's shop? He must have silver to hold his food!

He ordered his advisors to find the thieves who had taken his silver and make certain that each and every piece was returned at once! The advisors questioned the servants, the ladies-in-waiting, and the guards, but no one had seen the king's silver. Then one of the advisors made a small suggestion.

"Sire, a great wizard has come to Seville. He is said to know a person's past and to see the future. Perhaps he can find your silver."

The king's eyes sparkled. The wizard sounded like just the man he needed, and his skills sounded entertaining as well. Without delay, he summoned Juan Miguel to the palace.

Juan Miguel bowed to the king and then stood nervously in his robe, his hands shaking under the long, wide sleeves. What would the king ask of him?

"So, you are Juan Miguel the Great," he chuckled. "You look like just a boy to me. But we shall see if you truly have magical powers, or if you are just a rascal."

"I shall use my skills to serve Your Majesty," Juan Miguel said. He didn't feel as brave as he did in the marketplace, and he worried that the king wouldn't be as easy to trick.

"Some knave has stolen the silver plates and goblets from the castle," the king began. "Not one of my advisors can find a trace of the thief. Since you see the past and the future, I command you to prove yourself by finding my silver."

Juan Miguel felt his throat tighten. He swallowed hard. "It might take some time, Your Highness." He swept his arm wide, gazing at everyone around the room. "I foresee that the silver will be found."

"Indeed it will," the king said, "or you will pay with your own life. And just to make the challenge interesting, you shall be locked in the dungeon. With your skills, that shouldn't pose a problem." Juan Miguel's knees began to knock together. But the king hadn't finished. "If you haven't found my silver in three days, you shall be punished as an example to anyone else who pretends to see the past and the future."

Guards marched Juan Miguel down dark corridors, further and further away from the

Great Hall. They unlocked a thick oak door studded with brass nails, and Juan Miguel was led down moss-covered stone steps, deep into a dank cellar.

An unshaven jailer rattled a large set of keys, each one bigger than Juan Miguel's wrist bone, and shoved him into an empty cell. There was a hard bench for a bed and a small table. The jailer slammed the door of the cell behind him and turned the key in the lock. High above him, Juan Miguel saw a bit of sunlight pouring through a small, grated window. He blinked his eyes in the dim cell.

"I have brought this upon myself with all my trickery," he thought. "If only I can find a way out of this, I shall return to my mother and work hard to help her. How I have wasted my life."

Daylight faded, and still Juan Miguel had not thought of a way out of his plight. How could he discover who had stolen the king's silver while he was locked in the dungeon? He felt faint with hunger, for he had had neither food nor water all day. Just then, the jailer turned the key, and a servant came in bearing a tray of food. There was a bowl of thin

porridge, a few crusts of stale
bread, and a mug of water.

"At the inn where I stayed,
I was given the tastiest fare the
cook could prepare," he said.

"Just be glad you have been
sent any food at all," the servant
commented. He set the tray on
the rickety table, and turned to go.

Juan Miguel sighed. A full day had passed,
and he had only two days left. He glanced at
the darkening window and said softly,

> *The day is gone, as is the sun.*
> *Of all three, there goes one.*

The servant looked alarmed, and nearly
ran from the cell. Up the stairs he bounded,
as if the jailer were chasing him. He huddled
in the pantry with two other kitchen servants.

"It's true that Juan Miguel can see a man's
past," he whispered. "When I brought his
food, he knew that I was one of three thieves
who has taken the silver! We must confess and
beg him to save us from the king's wrath."

But his friends didn't believe him. "You are
imagining things," one said.

"No one can see a person's past," said the

other. "I will bring his food tomorrow, and test him again."

By the end of the second day, Juan Miguel had nearly given up hope. As hard as he tried, he could not think of a plan to save himself. He hoped the king would lift his sentence, and tell him it had only been a joke.

But when the servant brought his poor supper, Juan Miguel saw the light fade from the window. Two whole days had come and gone. He sighed,

"The sun has set,
and so it's true.
Of the three,
I've now seen two."

The second servant ran from the cell and raced up the stairs to find his companions. They hid in an empty room.

"We are discovered!" he lamented. Sweat beaded upon his forehead. "The great wizard knows that I am also a thief! We must confess and beg him to save us!"

But the third thief was not convinced. "You are both imagining things," he scoffed. "You are so filled with guilt that you just imagine you are caught. No man can see another's past. Tomorrow I shall bring the wizard his food, and prove it to you."

Poor Juan Miguel knew nothing of this. He sat alone in his cell on the third day.

"If only I had been more help to my family," he thought. "If only I had tried to be clever in making an honest living, I wouldn't be here now." He tried to think of some way to save himself, but all his ideas seemed to have flown out the window like so many tiny gnats.

That evening, Juan Miguel wasn't hungry. He was so worried about the punishment that would come the next morning, he didn't think he could swallow a crumb, even if the king had sent a plate of delicious food.

When the third servant brought a tray of food, he stared. Juan Miguel thought the servant felt sorry for him. He gave a great sigh, and said,

"If only my mother were here with me,
I'd tell her that now I've seen all three."

The servant was shocked at Juan Miguel's words. He ran out of the cell and straight to his thieving friends.

"We are found out!" he cried. "We must go to Juan Miguel and beg forgiveness, or tomorrow we will die in his place."

Each of the men took a plump piece of fruit from the kitchen and pretended it was for the wizard's last night on Earth. But when they entered his cell, they fell to the floor and begged him not to tell the king what they had done.

"If you spare us," said the first, "we will serve you for the rest of your days."

"If you spare us," said the second, "we will never question your wisdom."

"If you spare us," said the third, "we will speak of your great powers to everyone we meet."

Juan Miguel hid his surprise and

pretended he had expected this to happen. He narrowed his eyes and looked down upon the three servants groveling at his feet.

"First, you must collect the stolen silver, and bring it to this cell tomorrow morning. Let no one see you." The servants nodded their heads as they kneeled on the cold dirt floor.

"Next, you must never steal again. If you do, I will know and see that you are punished severely. And finally, you must do my bidding for the rest of your days."

"We agree," they promised.

The next morning, the king summoned Juan Miguel. The jailer and the guards marched him up from the empty dungeon, through the long corridors, and into the Great Hall.

The king smiled. "So, have you found my silver?"

Juan Miguel bowed low. "The silver lies in the cell I have just left," he said, "but the thieves are far from here and will not be found."

The king sent his servants down to the dungeon, and they returned carrying silver plates, goblets, and bowls. They placed the silver at the foot of the king's throne.

"I wouldn't have believed it," said the king. "Truly, you are a great wizard. Tell me your greatest wish, and it shall be granted."

Juan Miguel fell to his knees. "If it pleases Your Majesty," he said, "I only desire to return to my family and live a humble life." Then he added, "It would be of great service to me if the three servants who brought me my food while I was imprisoned could join me on my journey."

The king gave a great laugh and tossed Juan Miguel one of his heavy silver goblets. "Your wish is modest. Take this goblet as a remembrance of how you have served your king."

Juan Miguel stepped out into the courtyard. The sun shining on his face seemed a beautiful gift. The fresh air gave him pleasure. The three servants appeared, each leading a burro laden with gifts for Juan Miguel and his family.

The thieves served Juan Miguel faithfully all their days, telling the villagers tales of his deeds, though none of them were true. They prepared wonderful meals, did the washing, and kept the house clean. Juan Miguel's mother rested under the shade of a tree and praised her eldest son. And so it was that clever Juan Miguel, not quite a great wizard, fulfilled his promise to return to his family with enough wealth to care for them all.

The Twelve Months

Long ago, during a freezing Russian winter, at the edge of a tiny village, lived an orphan named Katya. She had been taken in by a woman named Ludmilla, and her daughter Dobrina. Although Dobrina was pretty enough, she was selfish, and always wore a scowl on her face. Neither Ludmilla nor Dobrina did any work at all. Instead, they gave orders to Katya.

No matter how hard Katya worked, she never complained, for she was grateful to have a roof over her head. Katya was a rosy-cheeked girl with a rosy outlook on the world, as well. She sang as she milked the cow and fed the chickens. She hummed while she swept the house, cooked the meals, and washed clothes. Katya worked long after the woman and her daughter were asleep in their warm beds. Then she would curl up on a straw pallet near the stove and dream of a better life.

One bitter cold evening, Dobrina moved closer to the fire that Katya had built. "Tomorrow is my birthday," Dobrina said. "How I would love a bouquet of sweet-smelling violets."

Ludmilla turned to Katya and said, "Go into the forest, child, and do not return until you have collected violets to celebrate Dobrina's special day."

Katya peered through the ice designs that curled around the windowpane. The ground was deep with snow, and wind rustled through the trees.

"But it is January," she said. "There are no violets now. You must wait for spring, and then I shall gladly gather a big bouquet."

"If my Dobrina wishes it," Ludmilla said, "you shall do it." She pushed poor Katya out the door, and as she closed it against the cold, she said, "Do not come back without the violets."

Katya had nothing to keep her warm but a thin shawl, which she pulled around her head and shoulders. There was nothing to be done. She trudged through the deep snow toward the darkening forest. Snow covered every path, and the trees closed out every bit of light. She couldn't see a sliver of moonlight or a single shining star. Before long, Katya's feet grew numb in her thin shoes. Her fingers were stiff with cold. But still, she climbed higher into the forest. It doesn't matter where I go, for I shall surely freeze to death before I ever see a violet, she thought.

Then Katya saw a light ahead of her. It

flickered and glowed. Then she smelled the smoke of a wood fire. Climbing higher, she approached a clearing in the forest where a huge bonfire blazed with warmth. Around the fire stood twelve men, all finely dressed in warm cloaks with hoods pulled over their heads. Three of the men wore capes as white as the snow that blanketed the ground. Three wore cloaks as green as a spring meadow. Three others were draped in golden brown, like fields of ripe grain. The last three were covered with flowing capes the color of ripe purple grapes. The twelve men talked amongst themselves, and barely noticed the small girl who came near.

"Excuse me," she interrupted in a soft voice. "I am so cold. Please, may I warm myself by your fire?"

The men turned to look at the girl. An old man clutching a tall wooden staff stepped forward. Katya was frightened, but she was so cold she couldn't bear to turn away from the fire's warmth.

"What are you doing in the forest on this cold night?" asked the old man. Long white hair flowed from his head, and his thin white beard moved up and down as he spoke. Katya realized that this must be Old January, and the men around him were all the other months of the year. She bowed respectfully.

"I have come to pick violets. Please, sirs, do you know where I might find some?"

"Violets in January?" the old man bellowed. "What a foolish idea! Do you expect to find violets growing underneath the snow?"

Katya shook her head. "Of course not," she said, "but the woman who cares for me sent me out because her daughter wants violets for her birthday. I can't return without them." Tears began to well up in her eyes. "Then I must stay here until March."

A young man cloaked in green stepped forward. "Lend me your staff, Old January," he said.

"Impossible!" the old man said gruffly to the man in green. "March cannot come before February!" But the young man held out his hand. Old January sighed and handed him the staff.

Brother March stepped forward and stirred up the fire with the long staff. The flames rose higher, and Katya felt as if she were cloaked in its heat. The snow around her began to melt. Red buds swelled on the bare tree branches, grass sprouted under her feet, and a blanket of tiny plants unfolded from their winter sleep. Their blossoms began to open, and soon Katya saw a blaze of violets all about.

"Hurry, my child," Brother March called to her. "Gather your violets before spring spreads throughout the forest." Katya picked a handful of the delicate flowers, smelling their sweet fragrance.

"This will be more than enough," she said, and thanked the Twelve Months for their help. Before she turned to go, Old January handed her a small pair of fur-lined boots and a thick cloak.

"Dress warmly before you leave," he said. "When you return to the village, do not let the woman and her daughter find these."

Katya bowed again and ran from the forest. When she reached the farmhouse, she hid the cloak and the boots in the back of the chicken coop. Then she banged on the door.

When Ludmilla opened it, Katya handed her the violets. Imagine Dobrina's surprise when she saw the bouquet before her! She took the flowers and breathed in their perfume. Then she tucked them into a pocket on her dress, without a word of thanks.

"How did you find violets in the middle of winter?" Ludmilla sputtered.

"There was a blanket of them on the mountainside," Katya said. "I only had to pick them."

Dobrina turned to her angrily. "Then why didn't you pick more?" The next afternoon, as she sipped tea and ate some sweet bread Katya had baked, Dobrina began to complain.

"It's so long until summer. How I would love a bowl of strawberries!" As soon as Dobrina wished for them, Ludmilla had to have them for her spoiled daughter. She turned to Katya.

"You lazy, good-for-nothing girl," she said, "go into the forest and bring Dobrina some ripe strawberries."

"Where will I find strawberries in January?" Katya asked. "Surely, there are no strawberries under the snow."

"If Dobrina wishes it, you shall do it!" Ludmilla shouted. She thrust an empty basket at Katya and pushed her out the door. Katya felt her heart sink as she heard the heavy bolt slide into place behind her.

She took the boots and cloak that Old January had given her, and when she was out of sight of the farmhouse, she put them on. At least she would not freeze on her journey. Katya tried to follow the path her footsteps had left the night before. She had to return to the Twelve Months to find strawberries in January.

After a long climb through the cold air, Katya saw the bonfire of the Twelve Months

burning up ahead. She quickened her steps and entered the clearing. Katya bowed low to them.

"Excuse me for bothering you again," she said, "but my mistress has sent me on another impossible errand. Please let me warm myself by your fire for a little while."

Old January stepped toward her. "What are you seeking this time, child?"

"I must fill this basket with strawberries," she said. "Do you know where I can find some?"

"There are no strawberries in winter," the old man cried. "Do you think strawberries grow underneath the snow?" But this time, he turned to a man dressed in a golden cloak. He handed him the staff and said, "Brother June, this is up to you."

Brother June stepped closer to the fire and stirred the ashes. Warmth encircled Katya, and the snow began to melt, trickling down the mountainside. Grass sprouted beneath her feet, leaves burst forth on the trees, and birds began to sing. Plants with hundreds of little white blossoms sprang from the ground. Then the blossoms turned into sweet strawberries that grew and ripened before her eyes.

"Hurry," called Brother June. "Pick your strawberries before the birds return from the south."

Quickly, Katya filled the basket with the bright red strawberries. She walked around the circle, thanking each of the months in turn. When she reached Brother June, he handed her a small box.

"Inside this box are precious jewels. Do not show them to anyone, but keep them in a safe place. Someday they will help you start a new life," he said gently.

Katya hurried back to the farmhouse. She hid the cloak and boots in the chicken coop, and placed the treasure box under one of the hen's nests. She knew that Ludmilla and Dobrina would never look there.

Standing in her shawl and shoes, she banged on the door. When Ludmilla saw Katya standing before her holding a basket brimming with strawberries, she was nearly speechless.

"How did you get these?" Dobrina demanded, stuffing her mouth with the juicy berries.

"I found them up on the mountain, just where I picked the violets yesterday," she said. "There were hundreds of ripe strawberries, far too many to pick."

Ludmilla turned her back on Katya. "I'll bet you've already eaten your fill," she said. Then she joined her daughter and the two women ate every last strawberry in the basket, without so much as a word of thanks.

But Katya's troubles were still not over. The next day, after Katya chopped a pile of wood to feed the kitchen fire, Dobrina began to complain. "It's been so long since I tasted an apple. I can't wait until fall. I must have an apple or I think I shall die!"

That was enough for Ludmilla. She grabbed Katya and pushed her out the door, telling her not to return until she had found apples for Dobrina. Katya didn't even try to argue. She knew she must do whatever Ludmilla told her.

Katya took the cape and boots from the chicken coop, and put them on when she was out of sight of the farmhouse. She had not eaten any dinner, and her stomach rumbled with hunger. To keep up her spirits as she began the journey to the mountaintop, she sang into the darkness.

At last, when her legs felt so weary she thought she could not walk any farther, Katya saw the warm glow of the fire flickering through the trees. When she entered the clearing, Old January beckoned to her and made a place for her by his side.

"Have they sent you out into the night again?" he asked. "What have they demanded this time?"

"I must find apples," Katya explained, "for Dobrina likes them, and says she cannot wait until autumn."

Old January handed his staff to a gray-haired man wearing a deep purple cape. "Brother September," the old man said, "it is up to you."

"Come, child," Brother September said kindly, "let us find you some apples." He stepped toward the fire, and stirred it with the staff. At once the snow melted, running in rivulets under Katya's feet. Grass grew on the forest floor, and leaves on the trees burst forth in scarlet and yellow hues. Above her head, apples swelled on a leafy branch.

"Hurry," Brother September called. "Shake the tree!"

Katya shook the tree, and one red apple fell into her apron. She put it in her pocket and shook the tree again. Another apple fell into her hands. Then Brother September handed her a sack filled with dried seeds.

"Take these," he said, "and show them to no one. When you are your own mistress, you can sow them in your fields."

"Hurry home!" Old January cried.

Katya bowed to the Twelve Months, thanked them again for all their help, and climbed back down through the forest to the farmhouse.

When she showed herself at the door, Ludmilla was angrier than Katya had ever seen her. "This time you will tell us where you found these apples!"

Katya was so frightened, she told Ludmilla all about the Twelve Months, and how they had melted the snow and given her each thing she asked for.

"Did they give you anything else?" Ludmilla demanded.

"I didn't ask for anything else," Katya

answered. It was true. She wouldn't tell Ludmilla about the cloak, the boots, the box of jewels, or the bag of seeds. They were her secret treasures.

"What a silly girl you are," Dobrina said. "If I had found the Twelve Months, I wouldn't have asked for just a few violets, or one basket of strawberries, or two apples. I would have made the most of the chance. Can you imagine what people in the village would pay for fresh fruits and vegetables and flowers in January? Get my cloak and boots," she demanded. "I will go to the Twelve Months myself. Then you shall see how to ask for what you wish!"

Katya brought Dobrina's things, and the young woman bundled up against the cold. In spite of her mother's pleas to stay home by the fire, she took three big baskets from their pegs and set off on the snowy path.

Dobrina was cold, and her legs became tired. She was ready to give up, but then she saw the light of the fire glimmering through the trees.

"So, the girl told the truth!" she said to herself. She walked boldly into the circle and warmed her hands at the fire, without so much as greeting the Twelve Months. They stopped their talk and glared at her.

"Who are you, and what are you doing here?" Old January asked.

"My serving girl, that foolish Katya, told me this is where she found violets and strawberries and apples. I have come to fill my baskets with fruits and vegetables and flowers from the warm months. From you, June, I want the biggest, juiciest strawberries and raspberries! July, give me cucumbers and cabbages. August, from you I want blackberries. From you, September, apples and pears. And from you, October . . ." Old January silenced her with a wave of his staff.

"You must wait, like everyone else, for each of the months to take their turn in the proper order. This month is my month! I am still king!" Old January roared.

"I'm not talking to you, old man!" Dobrina said rudely. "My business is with the warm months. Mind your own business of ice and snow!" Then she turned her back on him.

"Indeed I shall!" Old January cried. He pointed his staff toward the sky, and a heavy snow began to fall. Wind whipped through the trees, bearing the snow like tiny pellets of ice. The fire began to die down, and then, with one last crackle, it went out.

Dobrina was alone in the darkness. She tried to make her way back to the path, but she was not used to walking in the forest and soon lost her way. Snow swirled around her.

In the farmhouse, Ludmilla went from window to door, peering into the night, watching for her daughter.

"Where could she be?" she worried. "My poor Dobrina!" Hours passed, and soon the woman became so concerned that she put on her cloak, wrapped her head in a wool scarf, put warm boots on her feet, and headed off into the darkness to search for her daughter.

Katya was alone in the house while the storm raged outside. She fed the fire with logs to keep herself warm. She ate the supper she had made. She watched from the window, but saw no sign of Ludmilla or her daughter.

The next morning, the storm had ended. Sun glistened on the fresh snow. The trees seemed to sparkle as if they were lit with candles. Katya fed the chickens, milked the cow, and waited. But Ludmilla and her daughter did not return that day, or the next, or in the days and weeks after that.

Katya became mistress of the farmhouse. In time, she married a young man from the village and had children of her own. They always lived well, and none questioned why, for Katya and her husband were hard workers and kept their farm in perfect order. And every spring and summer, everyone who passed by said that her garden was the most beautiful and the most bountiful in all of Russia.

Brer Rabbit and Brer Bear

Brer Rabbit was about as clever as any rabbit around. He knew how to feed himself without ever doing a lick of work. He knew just when to sneak into Brer Fox's vegetable patch and pull out the sweetest carrots. He knew when Brer Bear was frying up a pile of fresh fish, and would walk in the door just in time to be invited for supper. There were strawberry patches ripe for the picking, and hickory nuts that would just fall into his hands.

But pretty soon, Brer Rabbit had a wife and a brood of children, and he knew he might need to do some farming of his own if he was going to feed them all. The first year, he planted the fields around his house. But the soil was sandy, and the crops were poor.

Early one spring, Brer Rabbit decided to find a good field to plant. He sauntered down the road, whistling into the midday sunshine, and turned in at the path leading to Brer Bear's. He knew the lumbering old bear had an empty field, and Brer Rabbit aimed to rent it, hopefully for nothing.

Brer Bear was sitting on his porch when he saw Brer Rabbit coming up the path. Brer Bear was instantly on the alert, for the wily rabbit had tricked him more times than he could count. He wasn't going to fall into another trap.

"Mornin'," Brer Rabbit called, pretty as you please. "Spring is coming, and isn't it fine?"

Brer Bear eyed Rabbit with suspicion. "What are you up to?" he asked.

"I've come to sit and talk a little business," Brer Rabbit said. "I've been eyeing your empty land. It's a good field for me to grow some crops, if you'd be willing to let me use it."

It was true Brer Bear didn't need the field, and hadn't plowed it for years. But why should he just turn it over to Brer Rabbit? His eyes narrowed.

"Now, that doesn't sound like a business proposition to me," he declared. "But I might consider letting you rent the field. If the price was right."

Well, paying Brer Bear was the last thing on Brer Rabbit's mind. He didn't have a copper penny to his name. But he played it cool.

"Why, that would be one good way to do it," he said. He smoothed the whiskers on his cheeks. "Probably a lot cheaper than what I was thinking of offering."

A frown creased Brer Bear's forehead. He had to be careful not to fall for another trick. But maybe there was a better way to profit from letting Brer Rabbit use his land. He settled into his rocking chair, rocked back and forth slowly, and tried not to look too interested in what Brer Rabbit had in mind.

"I think one hundred dollars would be more than fair," Brer Bear said.

Brer Rabbit didn't blink. "It sure would," he agreed. "Just one hundred dollars to rent that entire field? Is that all? Well, I'll be!" He extended his hand, ready to shake on the deal.

This made Brer Bear very nervous. Why would Brer Rabbit agree to the price he asked so quickly? It must be too little to ask in rent. Maybe Brer Rabbit planned to offer more than Brer Bear had asked.

He held his hand back. "Not so fast," he

said. "You said you came to talk business. So you might as well tell me what you had in mind."

"Oh no," Brer Rabbit stammered. "Your offer is plenty fair. I know that's a fertile piece of land, and I'm ready to get it under the plow today." He looked down at the ground and shook his head. "My plan was nothing. Nothing at all." He held out his hand again. "Shall we shake on the deal?"

Now Brer Bear was certain he was being played for a fool. "The deal is off," he said. "You might as well tell me what you came to offer." He rocked a little faster.

"You sure drive a hard bargain," Brer Rabbit said, fluffing out his tail. He sighed as if he were completely defeated. "All right, then. I was going to offer to share crops with you. That way, you'd have more food, with less work. I guess you could sell your share, too. It would probably be worth a lot more than just a puny hundred dollars. I reckon you've got me right where you want me now."

Brer Bear still felt a prickle of suspicion. But he was proud of himself for getting the rabbit to admit what his plan was. Brer Bear hadn't thought about sharing crops before.

"I'll rent you the land for one-half of the crops," Brer Bear announced.

"One-half?" Brer Rabbit exclaimed, hopping on one foot and then on the other. "And I suppose you want the top half, to boot!"

Now Brer Bear was confused. He had thought of taking half of whatever Brer Rabbit grew. He didn't think of it as being the top or the bottom. But he was willing to make this deal, too. Since he had his choice, he would make sure he got the better of Brer Rabbit this time around. "Why, I will take the top," he said, and held out his hand.

"Well, I don't know," Brer Rabbit mumbled to himself. He hemmed and he hawed and he pondered, and he wandered around the porch in little circles. Finally, he stopped right in front of Brer Bear's rocking chair.

"I give up," Brer Rabbit said, holding out his hand. "You win. I'll grow the crops, and you'll get the tops."

Brer Bear was only too glad to seal the partnership with a handshake. "Done," he said.

The next week, Brer Bear saw Brer Rabbit plowing the fields with his sons. He had never seen the rabbit work so hard. As for Brer Bear, he decided he could leave one of his other fields unplanted. After all, he would get half of Brer Rabbit's crops, right off the top.

In the summer he saw Brer Rabbit, with his wife and his children, pulling weeds from the field and caring for the plants like they were babies. They grew in perfect rows, all neat as you please. Brer Bear couldn't help but congratulate himself on the fine bargain he had made. He liked sharecropping.

As summer drew to a close, Brer Bear was pleased to see that Brer Rabbit's field was lush and green. The plants were bushy and full. He wasn't sure what the rabbit had planted, but his mouth was watering, waiting for the crop to be harvested.

At last the days cooled down, and the harvest moon rose in the sky. One morning, Brer Bear pranced down the road to the field, pushing a wheelbarrow in front of him. Brer Rabbit was going to be bringing in his crops today, and Brer Bear was planning to take his share. Down the road he went, singing softly to himself, "Taking the tops, I'm taking the tops."

When he got to the field, there was Brer

Rabbit, leaning against the fence and smiling up at Brer Bear. "Why, you're just in time," he said. "I'm ready to bring in this mighty fine crop of potatoes and yams. Where do you want your tops?"

"'Taters?" Brer Bear shouted. "You planted 'taters? Why, every last one of those 'taters is under the dirt! There's nothing on top but leaves!" Brer Bear was hopping mad, but he wasn't done with Brer Rabbit. Not by a long shot. "I know you've got something else growing, too," he said. "What's planted on the far side of my field?"

"Why, you get the tops of that crop, too, Brer Bear. I know you're no dunce, and I'd never cheat you out of your fair share. That crop down there is peanuts."

"Peanuts!" Bear shouted again. "Why . . . peanuts grow underground, too!" Well, Brer Bear was so mad, he couldn't even stay to argue. He left the wheelbarrow leaning against the fence and went stomping down the road, muttering to himself. "That rabbit! 'Taters and peanuts he planted! Just 'taters and peanuts!" He could hear Brer Rabbit laughing behind him all the way down the road.

The next spring, Brer Bear was still smarting from Brer Rabbit's sting, when along came the rabbit, pretty as you please, with another offer.

"I do apologize for the way things worked out last year," Brer Rabbit said. "I'm hoping you'll forgive my mistake. This year, if you let me sharecrop that field again, I'd be happy to give you the bottom half of everything I grow."

Brer Bear thought about the peanuts growing under the earth. He thought about potatoes and yams growing sweet and fat. He didn't want Brer Rabbit to take advantage of him again. But as he thought about the peanuts and yams, he could almost taste Brer Rabbit's harvest.

"You'll give me all the bottoms?" Brer Bear asked.

"Absolutely!" Brer Rabbit promised. "You'll get the bottoms of the whole crop." He held out his hand. Brer Bear thought he couldn't lose this year. At least Brer Rabbit was making up for what he had done. He held out his hand.

"It's a deal!" he agreed.

All through the spring, Brer Bear sneaked

up on the field to make sure that Brer Rabbit was plowing and getting the field ready. He saw the rabbit, sweat beading on his brow, as he pushed the plow through the soft earth. He saw Brer Rabbit sowing seeds in straight rows, up and down the field. Brer Bear smiled to himself.

In the summer, Brer Bear watched the weather. The rains came just when needed. The sun shone on the tall green plants. Pretty soon, Brer Rabbit's crop looked like it would be the best in the county.

Brer Bear was thinking of potato fritters, sweet yam pie, and mouthfuls of crunchy peanuts. When the harvest moon rose in the sky, Brer Bear hightailed it down to the field, and spent the night next to the fence. He didn't want Brer Rabbit to begin the harvest without giving him all the bottoms of the crop.

When the sun rose, Brer Rabbit came sauntering along the path, with his entire family in tow. They held tools and rolled a big wooden barrel in front of them, bumpety-bumping down the road.

"I see you're here to collect your share," Brer Rabbit said with a smile. "We'll have this field cut down in no time at all, and you can take all the bottoms home with you."

Brer Bear rubbed his hands together. He pushed his wheelbarrow into the field. "How did the yams do this season?" he asked.

"Yams?" Brer Rabbit asked. "Why, I didn't plant a single 'tater this year. The family was plumb tired of eating peanuts and 'taters all winter. I decided to make a change. This year I went to grain."

"Grain?" Brer Bear asked in a tired voice, knowing that nothing but roots would be at the bottoms of the plants. Visions of sweet yam pies and crunchy peanuts faded from his mind.

"Sure enough, Brer Bear," the wily rabbit said. "This year I've planted oats and barley. That way, we can make some fine soups and some tasty breads this winter. Nothing like a hot meal when the weather cools." He surveyed the field, while Brer Bear sagged against the fence. "I'll get these stalks of grain cut down right quick, and you can dig up the roots to your heart's content."

Brer Bear couldn't believe the rabbit had tricked him twice! Why hadn't he thought to

ask what crops Brer Rabbit was planting before he made his agreement to keep the bottoms? He made the mistake of thinking that Brer Rabbit would plant the same crop every year. As he walked home, Brer Bear could only imagine how empty his stomach would be this winter, while Brer Rabbit would be feasting on barley and oats.

By the next spring, Brer Bear was still angry about the way Brer Rabbit had tricked him. He wasn't going to let the rabbit use his fields again. There was no way he could make a profit on sharecropping with that pesky rabbit. He would have to plant all his fields himself if he didn't want to spend another hungry winter.

But by and by, as the sun warmed the earth, Brer Rabbit walked up to Brer Bear's porch. He sat himself down on the railing as if nothing had ever happened between them.

"Mighty fine weather," Brer Rabbit commented. Brer Bear only nodded. "I'm thinking of getting the field ready for planting." He looked at Brer Bear. "That is, if you'll let me share my crop with you again this year."

Brer Bear couldn't believe the rabbit had the nerve to ask for another deal. "You've bamboozled me for the last time," he sputtered. "I won't share crops with you ever again! I'd rather let the field go to clover!"

But Brer Rabbit stayed calm. "Why, Brer Bear," he soothed, "it was you who struck the bargain. You asked for the bottoms, and I agreed." He gave a shrug. "Make me an offer."

Brer Bear eyed the rabbit with suspicion. "You're going to let *me* set the terms?" he asked. "In that case, I'll take the tops *and* the bottoms!" Brer Bear was thinking that whether Brer Rabbit planted root vegetables or grain, he would reap the profits.

"That's not fair at all!" the rabbit protested. "If you take the tops and the bottoms, what will that leave me?"

"You get the middles," Brer Bear announced. "Take it or leave it."

Brer Rabbit argued and bargained, but Brer Bear wouldn't change his mind. "I give up," Brer Rabbit said at last. "You sure drive a hard bargain. This year you get the tops and the bottoms, and I'll take the middles."

The rabbit held out his hand. Brer Bear hesitated for a minute, but feeling certain that he couldn't be tricked this time, he shook on the deal.

Peering through the bushes at the side of the field, Brer Bear spent lots of time spying on Brer Rabbit. He saw the rabbit plow the field in the spring. He watched as he planted seeds from one end of each row to another. When the fields were parched, Brer Rabbit hauled in buckets of water from the spring and kept his plants growing. He and his family pulled out weeds and picked off bugs. By late summer, the crops were tall and green, waving in the breeze. Brer Bear wasn't sure what Brer Rabbit had planted, but how could he lose this time? He would take both the tops and the bottoms of the crops.

When the harvest moon rose high in the sky, Brer Bear raced down to the field to collect his share. With the first light of day, Brer Rabbit trooped down the path, followed by his missus and all his children, who were growing sturdy with the food Brer Rabbit had raised.

"Well, howdy do!" Brer Rabbit greeted him. Each of the children greeted the bear in turn, and the missus smiled sweetly. "Guess you're here to collect your share," he said.

"That I am," said Brer Bear firmly. "I'll take the tops and the bottoms this time, and won't be cheated again."

"You're surely welcome to them," Brer Rabbit said. "Just hold on until we take our middles. The rest of the field is yours."

Brer Bear licked his lips. "What did you plant this time?" he asked. "Peanuts, 'taters, oats, or barley?"

Brer Rabbit sauntered into the rows of plants and said, "This year, I've gone to corn!" And Rabbit began picking the fat ears of corn that grew right in the middle of each plant.

Pacal and the Ants

Pacal was the youngest of three brothers. While they were tall and strong, Pacal was small and slender as a reed. He loved to watch the birds flitting through the trees and the clouds skittering across the blue Mexican sky. His mother called him a dreamer. His father called him lazy. But his brothers called him a fool.

"You have the name of a king," they teased, "but the brain of a kingfisher!" It was meant as an insult, of course, but Pacal had watched the tiny kingfisher bird and seen how clever and skilled it was. It could spy a fish underwater from the branch of a tree, and dive like a bolt of lightning to catch it for dinner.

One day, Pacal's eldest brother left home to seek a wife. Soon, he sent word that he had married the daughter of a farmer in a nearby village. He said he would stay and work the fields of his new family for one year. Then he would return home with his wife.

Pacal's father sighed. "It is right that your brother should take a wife," he said, "and he ought to spend time working for her family. I hope they will make a farmer of him. I have never been able to get a full day's work out of him. But, as little as he did, we will now have more work to do. There must be no more daydreaming, Pacal."

But whenever Pacal was in the fields, he couldn't help but watch the jewel-colored hummingbirds dart into the flowers. He had to follow the bees as they gathered pollen and brought it inside their hollow logs to make sweet honey. His brother grumbled and called Pacal a fool who was good for nothing.

Before long, the second brother left to seek his fortune. He sent word that he had married a younger sister in his brother's new household. He, too, would work for his new wife's family for one year.

Pacal was glad to be rid of his teasing brothers. But his father only sighed more deeply. "It is right that your brother should leave home to marry. And it is good that he will work his bride's fields. Perhaps her father might make a farmer of him. I know I had no luck with him. Still, there will only be more work for us, Pacal. No more time for daydreaming."

Pacal tried to keep his mind on the fields. But he couldn't help watching a green snake slither underneath a rock. He had to stop to listen to the multicolored parrots squawk to each other in the morning sun.

At last Pacal's father told him that it was time to follow his brothers and seek his own fortune in the world. Pacal's mother cried and hugged her youngest son.

"He is not old enough to take a wife and leave us," she told her husband. But Pacal's father would not change his mind.

"Let him go to a different village and do a year's work for another man. He will grow stronger and learn to pay attention to his work. Perhaps when he returns he will be more helpful to us here."

Pacal's mother tied up a bundle of food for his journey. Into a bright woven cloth she placed a few tortillas and a small earthen jar of thick corn paste.

"When you come to a stream," she told

him, "mix yourself some corn soup by adding water to the jar."

Pacal kissed his mother good-bye. He turned his back on the round thatched hut that had been his home and set off along the rough path. He didn't know where he was going or what he would do, but he promised himself he would show his family that he was more than a foolish dreamer.

At noon, he found a shady spot to stop and eat his lunch. Then Pacal slept until the sun had lost some of its midday heat. On he traveled until he came to a small village.

"I might ask for some supper and a place to sleep tonight," he thought, walking toward a hut that looked just like his own home. Imagine his surprise as he saw his two brothers enter just before him.

"Brothers!" he called. They greeted him, and Pacal joined them for a supper of chili peppers and beans with fresh tortillas. His brothers' wives were kind and pleasant, and they had one more sister in the household. She had a shy smile and eyes that twinkled.

The next day, Pacal followed his brothers to the fields, but he soon wandered away and sat

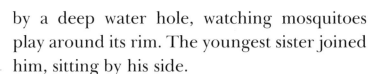

by a deep water hole, watching mosquitoes play around its rim. The youngest sister joined him, sitting by his side.

"I am called Pepita," she said, "'the little seed.' I am smaller than my sisters, but I am good at grinding corn and frying up crisp tortillas." Pacal smiled and remembered the delicious tortillas he had eaten the night before.

Days passed, and still Pacal remained with his brothers at the family's hut. He and Pepita wandered the fields and paths, catching butterflies and then setting them free. At last he asked her father for permission to marry his youngest daughter.

Pepita's father scowled. "You are scrawny and small. You aren't strong like your brothers. Instead of helping in the fields, you wander about as if there was no work to be done. I can't afford a son who will do nothing."

But Pacal promised he would work hard and bring honor to Pepita's family. At last her father agreed, the two were married, and Pacal dreamed of making them all proud.

As the spring earth warmed under the sun, Pepita's father lined up the three brothers. "We must have new fields for planting," he said. "Go into the forest and find a good piece of land. Then cut down the trees." He gave a hatchet to each of Pacal's older brothers, but did not offer a tool to Pacal. "Why bother," he said, "when you aren't strong enough to cut down a bush?"

Pepita's mother gave each of Pacal's brothers a bulging sack of tortillas and corn paste. But she didn't give anything to Pacal. "You won't work hard enough to deserve even one tortilla."

As Pacal walked down the path, alone and empty-handed, his new wife stepped out from behind a banana tree. "I know you will help with the new fields." She smiled and handed Pacal a cloth filled with warm tortillas and some dried corn.

When Pacal reached the forest, he saw his brothers searching for a piece of flat land. But every bit of land was covered with trees.

"I will help you cut down the trees," Pacal offered, but his brothers only chased him off.

"Find your own field," they yelled. "We don't need a daydreamer to get in the way and eat our dinner."

Pacal walked further into the forest until he

found himself on a white stone path. It led him past spectacular vine-covered pyramids, rising toward the sky. He walked under a carved stone arch.

"Why, I must be in a lost city of my Mayan ancestors," he marveled. A feeling of mystery hung over the spectacle of stone and jungle. "Perhaps I can find a place to make new fields here." But without any tools, he did not know how he would cut a single tree. At last, he stopped to rest on a crumbling stone step and eat a tortilla. The long walk had made him hungry. As the sun beat down upon his head, he set his last tortilla and the corn aside and curled up to rest. Soon he was fast asleep.

When Pacal opened his eyes, the sun was setting, and long shadows crept out from alongside the buildings in the abandoned city. The whole day had gone by, and he hadn't cut a single tree. As he reached down for his food bundle, Pacal saw a long line of leaf-cutter ants carrying pieces of his meal away.

"Now I shall have nothing to eat as well!" He followed the ants as they marched along under their heavy burdens. At last he arrived at the entrance hole to the ants' nest.

"Queen Ant!" he shouted down. "Come up here and see what your subjects have done to a poor husband."

A large ant, dressed in a dewy crown and a robe of glistening cobwebs, crawled from the hole and faced Pacal.

"Your workers have taken my food," he accused. "How can I clear a field for planting without a morsel to eat? You must repay me!"

The queen turned her head this way and that, sizing up Pacal. For the first time, he felt bigger than any other man on Earth.

"My workers need to feed the colony," she

said. "However, in return, we will clear your field for you."

Pacal couldn't believe what the queen of the ants had offered. If the ants could cut down the trees to clear a field for planting, a few tortillas would be a small price to pay. He quickly agreed. He picked some avocados and bananas to fill his stomach, then curled up to sleep as the stars twinkled like Pepita's eyes.

When he awoke, a large field had been cleared. Trees were stacked along the edges of the forest. Pacal watched the last of a long line of ants marching down into their nest. He knocked three times near the entrance to the nest. When the queen greeted him, Pacal bowed low and thanked her for her help. Then he strode back through the forest, whistling as he walked.

Along the way, he passed his brothers, who were hard at work with their hatchets. In each tree they made one deep slash, then moved on to the next. It seemed they thought that their father-in-law merely wanted them to make one cut in a tree, rather than cut the trees down. Pacal shook his head at their foolishness and kept walking.

When he returned to the hut, Pepita's father shouted at Pacal. "Are you back so soon? Since you haven't cleared a field, then you won't eat at my table!"

Pepita ignored her father's words and cooked a few tortillas, then gave her husband a bowl of corn soup.

Soon, Pacal's brothers came into the hut, sweating and full of complaints. Their wives fussed over them. The farmer praised their hard work and ordered chickens to be cooked to make them a hearty meal.

The next morning, Pepita's father lined up the three brothers. "Go out and burn the cut trees and the brush so the fields will be rich for planting."

The women gave Pacal's two older brothers a basket filled with food to take with them. They offered nothing to Pacal.

But once again, as he traveled along, far behind his brothers, Pepita stepped out from behind a tree and handed her husband a basket filled with fresh tortillas, corn soup, and a small pot of sweet honey. She beamed at him as he headed off.

This time, Pacal went straight to the queen

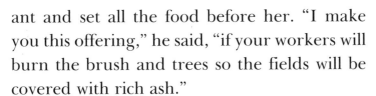

ant and set all the food before her. "I make you this offering," he said, "if your workers will burn the brush and trees so the fields will be covered with rich ash."

Then he went and sat under the shade of a stone archway. Millions of ants paraded in a long line, setting fires across the brush that covered the field, and burning the trees piled at its edges. Pacal's stomach growled, but he smiled with all his heart.

At the end of the day, he walked back along the white path, through the forest, and past his brothers, who were vainly trying to set fire to the green wood of the trees they had slashed the day before. A thin column of smoke rose into the air.

When he returned to the hut before his brothers, Pepita's father shouted at him. "You lazy bones! I saw a thin wisp of smoke coming from your field, while a huge cloud of smoke from your brothers' field nearly blocked the sun."

When the brothers arrived, two more chickens were cooked, and the brothers were treated with great respect.

The next day, the farmer lined up the

three brothers. He gave each of the two older brothers a mule loaded with baskets of corn seed. To Pacal, he gave just one small sack. Off they went to plant rows of corn. When Pacal passed his brothers, they were carelessly dropping a few seeds between the charred trees that dotted their field.

Pacal walked until he came to the leaf-cutters' nest once again. He placed his small sack of corn seed at the opening, and called the queen.

"Today the fields must be planted," he said. "But this is all the seed my wife's father has given me." Pacal told how much his brothers had been given and the condition of their field.

The queen pointed behind Pacal. "The fire spread beyond the field we cleared," she said. "Now there is a great deal of land to be planted. If you give us a portion of the seed to keep for ourselves, we will find a way to sow the corn."

Pacal agreed. He left the sack of seed for the queen, and went off to sleep under the shelter of stone. When he awoke, he saw thousands of worker ants traveling from his brothers' field to his own, each one balancing a corn seed upon its back. As far as he could see, ants swarmed across the land, dropping seeds into the rich earth. Pacal didn't forget to thank the queen for all her help before he left, and promised her a portion of the crop when it was harvested.

Through the spring and into the summer, Pepita's father scolded Pacal. Each evening, his brothers were given large portions of food, while Pacal was given little. But each day he promised his wife that all would turn out well. When at last it was time to harvest the corn, the farmer lined up the three brothers.

"Build an earth oven at the edge of your field and roast the young ears of corn," Pepita's father instructed them. "Then load the baskets upon these donkeys, and we will bring it home."

Each brother left, leading a donkey with two huge baskets. To Pacal, the farmer handed one small handbasket, then laughed and said, "This should hold everything your field has grown!"

The next day, Pacal watched as the farmer, his wife, and his daughters arrived at the brothers' field. A small earth oven held the few scrawny ears of corn his brothers had harvested.

"What's this?" cried the farmer in dismay. "Is this all you have to show for your work? What will we eat all winter?"

But Pacal told them to follow him to his fields. They walked along, through the forest, along the white road, past the pyramids, and finally to the top of a low hill. "Where is your earth oven?" the farmer demanded.

"Why, you are standing upon it, my father," said Pacal. Then he led the family to a mountain of roasted corn.

"Here is my harvest," he said.

During the moonlit night, the ants had built the earth oven and had picked and cleaned the corn. Pacal slept while it roasted in the oven, and then watched his helpers pile it up.

Back and forth went the family from Pacal's fields to the hut, loading up the baskets and leading the donkeys behind them. That night, they held a celebration in honor of Pacal. The entire village was invited. In the morning, the farmer sent Pacal's brothers back, along with their wives, to Pacal's own family. But the villagers built a new hut for Pacal and Pepita, right next to her parents.

Each day, Pacal ate his wife's tasty tortillas and her delicious roasted chicken. Each day, he smiled at the sparkle in her brown eyes. Soon, he taught his own children to help the ants tend the fields, and never scolded when they stopped to watch the world as it flitted and buzzed and sang around them. And he always brought food to the queen of the ants, to insure her help in planting the crops, year after year.